# WHO COMES TO THE WATER HOLE?

# WHO COMES

COBBLEHILL BOOKS
Dutton
New York

# TO THE WATER HOLE?

**Colleen Stanley Bare**
Photographs by the author

*To Grant*

Copyright © 1991 by Colleen Stanley Bare
All rights reserved. No part of this book may be reproduced in any form without permission in writing from the Publisher.

Library of Congress Cataloging-in-Publication Data

Bare, Colleen Stanley.
 Who comes to the water hole? / Colleen Stanley Bare ; color photographs by the author.
   p.   cm.
 Summary: Text and photographs examine the various animals that come to a water hole in Southern Africa during the dry season, including a white rhinoceros, yellow-billed stork, and hyena.
 ISBN 0-525-65073-3:
 1. Mammals—Africa, Southern—Juvenile literature.  2. Birds—Africa, Southern—Juvenile literature.  [1. Zoology—Africa, Southern.  2. Jungle animals.]  I. Title.
 QL731.S63B37  1991
 599.0968—dc20    91-7915 CIP AC

Published in the United States by Cobblehill Books,
an affiliate of Dutton Children's Books,
a division of Penguin Books USA Inc.

Designed by Charlotte Staub
Printed in Hong Kong   First Edition
10 9 8 7 6 5 4 3 2 1

It is the dry season in Southern Africa. No rain has fallen for several months, and the animals and birds are thirsty for water.

The plains and grasslands of the bush country stretch for thousands of miles, flat and sunbaked. Without rain, the once soft soil has dried and hardened. Tangles of brush and grassy growth have turned from green to brown, and many of the trees have dried-up leaves.

In this harsh, parched land is a haven, a refuge. It is a water hole fed by a spring. Here the trees stay green and the earth soft. Many kinds of animals and birds gather at the water hole, in ones, twos, threes, often more. They come to drink and drink and drink.

This mother WHITE RHINOCEROS drinks for a long time. She weighs about three thousand pounds — a lot of rhino to fill. OXPECKER birds, nicknamed TICK BIRDS, sit on her back and head. The birds feast on rhino ticks, flies, and other bugs.

The mother rhino's baby laps a little, looks around, laps and looks. The baby rhino still nurses and gets milk from its mother, so it doesn't need as much water.

Rhinos in Africa are very endangered. They are being killed by humans, called *poachers*, for their horns. The horns are used for making knife handles and medicines. Soon the only rhinos left in the world may be in zoos.

Wild pigs called WARTHOGS rush to the pond on short stubby legs. Sometimes they use their long tusks to dig up roots in the water, which they eat. Their shorter, sharper lower tusks are weapons for fighting.

Other animals also stand in the water, eating tender shoots and grasses. One is the BABOON. Baboons come to the water hole in large groups called *troops,* to drink and to eat.

A baby baboon hangs on while its mother drinks. Another baboon watches from a tree.

ZEBRAS approach the water hole cautiously, looking for predators such as lions, leopards, and hyenas. Although zebras are related to horses and are shaped like horses, their stripes make them unique. Only a zebra looks like a zebra.

The zebras line up to drink. A young zebra stands on the shore, watching.

Many kinds of antelope come to the pond. All of the males, called *bucks*, have horns which they use for fighting with other bucks. Female antelopes, known as *cows*, sometimes look very different from the bucks.

NYALA antelopes arrive in small groups. The hornless, finely striped tan cows are much smaller than the dark shaggy bucks.

A nyala buck tries to cut in on the drinking cows. The cows refuse to move, so he must go to the end of the line.

WILDEBEEST cows and bucks both have horns and look alike, except the cows are smaller. Wildebeests are antelopes that often travel long distances, in large herds, to find food and water.

IMPALA antelopes have tufts of black hair just above the hind hooves. Impala cows do not have horns.

The dignified-looking WATERBUCK antelope has a round ring of white fur on its rear. Waterbucks often stand in the water for hours, feeding on grasses and reeds.

Antelopes frequently stay close to the water hole. They eat and drink during the day and sleep in nearby brush at night.

These ROAN and SABLE antelopes are near the pond. The female roan has horns, but the buck's are much larger.
The SABLE buck antelope is dark and graceful.

This KUDU buck and two cows are feeding near the water. Kudu bucks have handsome spiraled horns and dark shaggy coats, unlike the hornless, light-colored cows.

Many animals come regularly to the water hole. But sometimes a different visitor may wander in, perhaps from the drying river miles away. One is the HIPPOPOTAMUS, which spends its days in water, in ponds or rivers, and goes ashore at night to feed on grasses, leaves, and herbs.

A CROCODILE may find its way to the pond. It hides under the water and eats fish. Sometimes it grabs an unsuspecting drinking bird, baboon, or antelope in its powerful jaws.

Birds come to the water hole, to feed and drink. Some are storks. A YELLOW-BILLED STORK uses its long beak to find fish and frogs, insects and worms on the bottom of the pond.

Another stork, the HAMMER-KOP, sits sunning after fishing for its favorite frogs.

The WOOLLY-NECKED STORK hunts for large insects, frogs, and fish in marshy, shallow parts of the pond.

An OSTRICH, the largest of all birds, stops drinking to watch for enemies with its big dark eyes.

Daily dramas unfold on the banks of the pond. Two male IMPALAS lock horns in battle.

MONKEYS sit on a tree branch and groom each other. They remove the other's mites, ticks, and fleas.

Another monkey grooms its foot.

Sociable MONGOOSES greet each other. Small and quick, they like to eat insects.

A gray MEERCAT stands tall, looking for predators. Related to the mongoose, meercats dig deep burrows in the ground.

Three GIRAFFES peer through the treetops. Giraffes are the tallest of all animals, up to eighteen feet.

A herd of ELEPHANTS gathers in a nearby clearing, lingers awhile, and moves on. Other times they too come to the water hole to drink and to bathe.

Animals at the water hole are always watchful and wary, alert for enemies. A lion's distant roar, even the sound of rustling leaves, can cause the group to run.

Four major predators hunt in the area, often at night: the lion, leopard, cheetah, and hyena. Each is a meat-eating animal and must kill to live.

LION

LEOPARD

LIONS live in groups called *prides*, with the females doing most of the hunting.

LEOPARDS are more solitary and hunt alone. They often hide in trees and pounce on their victims from above.

CHEETAHS are the swiftest of all animals and, for a short time, can run up to sixty miles an hour.

HYENAS resemble dogs and frequently hunt in packs.

One day the rains begin. The dry season is ending. Now animals and birds no longer need to come to the water hole to drink. They can drink anywhere, from the many new ponds being filled with rainwater. For a few months the water hole is quiet. Nourished by heavy rains, it grows bigger and deeper, ready for the next drought and the return of the wildlife.

# LIST OF SPECIES

## *Animals*

| NAME | FAMILY |
|---|---|
| Baboon   (*Papio ursinus*) | Cercopithecidae |
| Cheetah   (*Acinonyx jubatus*) | Felidae |
| Crocodile   (*Crocodylus niloticus*) | Crocodylidae |
| Elephant, African   (*Loxodonta africana*) | Elephantidae |
| Giraffe, Reticulated   (*Giraffa camelopardalis reticulata*) | Giraffidae |
| Hippopotamus   (*Hippopotamus amphibius*) | Hippopotamidae |
| Hyena, Spotted   (*Crocuta crocuta*) | Hyaenidae |
| Impala   (*Aepyceros melampus*) | Bovidae |
| Kudu, Greater   (*Tragelaphus strepsiceros*) | Bovidae |
| Leopard   ((*Panthera pardus*) | Felidae |
| Lion   (*Panthera leo*) | Felidae |
| Meercat   (*Suricata suricatta*) | Viverridae |
| Mongoose, Dwarf   (*Helogale parvula*) | Viverridae |
| Monkey, Vervet   (*Cercopithecus aethiops*) | Cercopithecidae |
| Nyala   (*Tragelaphus angasi*) | Bovidae |
| Rhinoceros, white   (*Ceratotherium simum*) | Rhinocerotidae |
| Roan antelope   (*Hippotragus equinus*) | Bovidae |
| Sable antelope   (*Hippotragus niger*) | Bovidae |
| Warthog   ((*Phacochoerus aethiopicus*) | Suidae |
| Waterbuck, Common   (*Kobus ellipsiprymnus*) | Bovidae |
| Wildebeest   (*Connochaetes taurinus*) | Bovidae |
| Zebra, Burchell's   (*Equus burchelli*) | Equidae |

## *Birds*

| | |
|---|---|
| Hammerkop (Hammerhead) Stork   (*Scopus umbretta*) | Scopidae |
| Ostrich   (*Struthio camelus*) | Struthionidae |
| Oxpecker (Tick bird)   (*Buphagus erythorhynchus*) | Sturnidae |
| Woolly-necked (White-necked) Stork   (*Ciconia episcopus*) | Ciconiidae |
| Yellow-billed Stork   (*Mycteria ibis*) | Ciconiidae |